Gulliver's Stories

Gulliver's Stories

**Retold from Jonathan Swift
by Edward W. Dolch,
Marguerite P. Dolch, and
Beulah F. Jackson**

Drawings by Jean-Jacques Vayssières

SCHOLASTIC INC.
New York Toronto London Auckland Sydney

ISBN 0-590-41842-4

12 11 10 9 8 7   4/9

Foreword

One of the all-time favorites among English stories is the famous Gulliver's Travels by Dean Swift. In fact the stories of Gulliver are so well told that after reading them one has the feeling that of course all these strange things really happened. That is the test of real literature, and that is why the popularity of these stories will never cease.

The Gulliver stories are so good in themselves that to enjoy them one does not need to know that actually Dean Swift was making fun of some of the things the people of England thought and did. For instance, Swift thought that wars were very foolish, and that is why he tells about the wars over which end of an egg to open first.

Swift got the idea for Gulliver's Travels because at that time many books were coming out telling of travels to strange parts of the world. Swift thought that he would make up some travels that would be stranger than any reported by anyone else. He certainly succeeded.

This book selects the first two of Gulliver's Travels, the one to Lilliput, the land of the little people, and the one to Brobdingnag, the land of the giants, because these are the most well-known and the most interesting. But it is hoped that the reader will find these stories so interesting that he will go to the whole volume of Travels and read the rest of the stories.

E. W. Dolch

Santa Barbara, California

Contents

Part II—My Voyage to Brobdingnag

PART I

My Voyage
to
Lilliput

I Find Myself
in Lilliput

I grew up in a small town in England with my four brothers. When I was old enough, my father sent me away to school. After I had been there three years, he found that it was costing him too much money. So I had to leave school.

I went to work for a doctor. I helped him with his work for four years. I

thought that I wanted to be a doctor. But I learned something else at the same time.

I loved the sea and after my work was done I read about sailing ships. I learned how to use the stars, the sun, and the moon to tell me which way to go, the way sailors do. I also learned other

things which would help me if I ever went to sea.

After I left the good doctor, I went to sea for three years as a doctor on a sailing ship. When I came back to London, I bought a small house in town and became a doctor there. I married and was very happy for a while. But soon I longed to go to sea again. I talked to my wife. Since it was all right with her, I went to sea again.

The ship on which I was sailing was to go to the South Seas. At first, things went very well. But as we came to a part of the world where the weather was very warm, many of the men became sick. I did the best I could for them, but twelve men died. The rest were still sick when a bad storm came up. We were driven on to a rock and our ship broke apart.

Some of us got a small boat over the side of the ship. We rowed as hard as we could, trying to reach shore. We rowed and rowed and rowed. We were still far from land but we were so tired we just had to rest. As we were resting, a big wave broke over us, upset our boat, and threw us all into the water.

I started swimming, but I was so tired I did not even look where I was going. When I thought I could not swim one more minute, I let my legs down. My feet touched bottom. I looked about and could see land ahead. I made my way to the land as best I could. I walked across the sand, and fell on my back on short, soft grass. I had never been so tired in all my life. I thought of nothing except how glad I was to be alive. I closed my eyes and went to sleep.

When I woke up, it was just getting light. I lay still for awhile, thinking about the things that had happened. I wondered where I was and where my friends from the ship were. Since I was hungry, I also wondered where I could find some food.

I thought I would get up and look around, but when I started to do so, I could not move! I tried to move my hands. They were tied to the ground with what felt like little strings. I tried to turn my head but my hair, which was long and thick, seemed to be tied to the ground. I could feel what felt like strings around my legs and my body. I could not move. I did not know what had happened to me. So I lay there quietly and listened.

I could see nothing but the sky. But I could hear a noise. It sounded like high, thin talking in a language I had never heard before.

Then I felt something. Something was moving up my left leg. When I tried to move, it would stop as if to see what I was going to do. Then, it would move again. I could also feel that some others were following after the first. I lay very still and waited until I could feel that the first one was nearly to my chin.

I could stand it no longer. I lifted my head until I thought I would pull every hair out by the roots. I turned my eyes down as much as I could. I looked down over my chin to see what was standing on my chest.

I could not believe my eyes! There stood a little man about six inches high! He was no taller than my hand. He carried a bow and held an arrow about as big as a pin. He was ready to shoot me with his bow and arrow!

I was so surprised to see that little man standing on my chest that I couldn't help laughing.

I let out my breath in a big, noisy laugh. The little man turned and ran. Those that I had felt following him all ran for their lives.

I stopped laughing as soon as I could and lay very still. I could hear them talking. Soon I felt them slowly coming back. One who must have been very brave used my ear for a step and climbed up so that he could get a good look at my face.

When he did this, he raised his hands and his eyes and said in a loud voice "Hekinah degul!" The others who were standing on my chest, afraid to come closer, each said the same words, two or three times. As I had never heard words like these before, I did not know what they meant. The little men did not sound unfriendly. Still I did not like the thought of being tied down. I began to try to move again.

Even though I was tied down by many, many little strings, I could still move a little. The little men must have felt as though they were standing on a ship at sea in a storm. They ran towards my legs as fast as they could go. Some fell down but they got up again and ran on. In just a minute they were all off my body.

My left arm did not seem to be tied quite as tightly as my right arm. I was very strong and I pushed on the ground with my fingers. When I did this, I heard the little men crying out. I felt some of the little strings break. Some little things that I found out later were pegs, flew out of the ground and hit me on the arm. But my left arm came free.

I lifted it at once to my head and tried to free my hair. I wanted to turn my head so that I could see and catch one of those little men. My hair was tied down so well that I could only turn my head about two inches.

I lifted and turned my head as much as I could. I looked towards my feet. There were no little men there but I soon found that they had not gone far. As I put my left hand up again to my hair, I heard one of them cry loudly, "Tolgo phonac!" Then I felt a hundred little needles prick my hand and my face.

I lifted my left hand to cover my face and found it was sticking full of little arrows such as I had seen the first little man carrying. Then I heard the same words again "Tolgo phonac!" and another lot of arrows hit me. I could also feel something at my side. It must have been the little men trying to drive their spears into my sides. But my clothes were so thick the spears did not hurt me.

The arrows in my hand and face hurt me. They burned like fire! I could not keep from crying out because of the pain. I lay still. As soon as I was still, they stopped shooting. So I lay very still and thought of what to do next.

Since I had one hand free, I was sure I could free the rest of me. But I could tell by the noises I heard that more and more of the little men were coming all of the time. I did not like the thought of being shot full of those needle-like arrows. So I just lay still and waited to see what would happen next.

CHAPTER II

I Am Taken
to the City

I had found that if I moved, the little men shot arrows at me that stung my hands and face. So I lay still to see what would happen. I did not have to wait long. I heard a knocking sound as though someone was building something. A little later, out of the corner of my right eye, I saw that the little men were building a kind of stand close to my head with ladders going up to it. It was about a foot and a half high so that it was above my face.

As soon as it was done, a little man, who was dressed much better than the others, climbed the ladders and stood near my face. He called to the others.

I could feel them cutting some of the strings on my hair on the left side so I could turn my head easily and look straight at the little man.

This man talked a long time. I did not know what he was saying because he used a language I had never heard before. But from the sound of his voice and the way he used his hands, and the look on his face, I could almost guess what he was saying. I felt sure he was trying to tell me that if I would not hurt any of his men and if I would do as they wanted me to do, they would not hurt me.

When he had talked quite a long while, he stopped and looked at me, and smiled. He waited as though he were now expecting me to speak.

So I did speak. I said I wanted to be friends and I waved my left hand around without touching any of the little men to show that I did not want to hurt them. I also told him that I was very hungry. Of course, he did not understand my words, but he seemed to know that I was friendly. When I put my hand up to my mouth and then acted as if I were eating, he knew at once what I wanted.

The well-dressed man, whom I later learned was called Turgo, turned and went down the ladders. The ladders were then taken down and placed against my body. Then up the ladders came little men carrying baskets. I later learned that the little men were the King's servants. The King had told the people to start cooking food for me as soon as he had heard about me. The men whom I first saw and who shot the arrows at me were the King's soldiers.

First, the servants gave me meat. I could not tell what kind it was by the taste. But it looked like roast sheep. I could see that the pieces were legs, though they were about as big as a bird's wing. And I could eat two or three in one bite. The meat was very good. I ate bones and all.

Some of the servants gave me loaves of bread, each about as big as a bullet, which I put into my mouth two or three at a time.

I was eating with my left hand. As fast as I emptied a basket, another little man would step up with another. But each one showed by his face how surprised he was at how big I was and how much I could eat.

I showed them that I was also thirsty. The little men let down some ropes and pulled up two of their biggest wine barrels. Each one was about half as big as one of our cups. They beat the tops of the barrels in and I picked them up and drank the wine in about two swallows. Somehow, this seemed to please them. They laughed and danced around on my chest. They cried again and again the same words the first little man had cried when he stepped up on my ear and looked at my face—"Hekinah degul!"

I could not help thinking that these little men were brave. With my free hand, I could have killed them all. But here they were dancing around on my chest. They did not seem at all afraid. My hand still hurt from their arrows, some of which were still in it. But even so, I felt friendly towards these little men. They had brought me as much food for one meal as all of them could eat in a week. They had laughed to see me eat it. "Yes," I thought, "these are brave little men!"

Soon after the little servants had given

me my breakfast that first day, I heard horns blowing. I could tell by the way the little men were acting that some very great person was coming. All the little men hurried down the ladders. They stood quietly around on the grass.

Then some little men came up a ladder which had been placed against my right leg. By turning my head as far to the right as I could, I watched the little men coming up to my face. There were about ten well-dressed men whom I knew were lords. They must be messengers from the King.

The leader climbed upon my face. He held a paper up to one of my eyes, so close I could not have read it even if I had known what the words said. Then he talked a long time. He seemed to be very friendly, for he smiled and bowed to me many times. He seemed to be trying to tell me something, for he kept pointing down the road. I lifted my head just a little and looked where he was pointing. I could see a beautiful little city, about half a mile away. I guessed that he was saying they were going to take me to the city.

When he was through speaking, I made a little talk too, even though I knew he could not understand me. I slowly lifted my free hand. I was careful that I did not move in a way that would upset him as he stood on my chest. I told him I would not hurt him or his men. But I showed him that I would like to be set free.

He understood me, for he shook his head "No." He made signs to tell me that they were going to take me to the city, lying down and tied. I tried to show him that I did not like this and made a few quick moves. But the minute I did this, I felt more of the little soldiers' arrows stick into my right hand and into my face. Since the arrows burned like fire, you can be sure I was soon quiet again.

When I was quiet, the little man and his friends walked down over me to the ladder against my leg and so down to the grass again. I could hear them talking. Then they went away.

I then felt the soldiers working on my right hand. They pulled out the arrows and rubbed on some good smelling medicine which made my hands stop hurting at once. Soon others were working on my face. They used my ears as steps to lift themselves high enough to pick out the arrows which had hit my face, and to rub on the medicine which stopped the hurting.

They also made the strings that tied me down a little looser so I could move a little more. This made me feel much better and I also began to feel very sleepy. I know now that the servants had put some medicine in the wine to make me sleepy. I must have slept the rest of the day and the night, too.

What the little men did while I was sleeping was told me afterwards when I had learned their language. The King had already said that I was to be brought to his chief city. His men had made ready a very long and wide wagon, with many wheels. The King had also told his servants to put something in my wine so that I would sleep very soundly. As I lay asleep, the little wagon was brought beside me. The strings were untied from the pegs in the ground. Then with many ropes and pulleys, and hundreds of men pulling on the ropes, I was lifted up and the wagon was pushed under me. Then I was let down on the wagon, still sleeping. I was again tied down, but this time to the wagon. Then hundreds of horses, each about four inches high, were hitched to the front of the wagon. The wagon was pulled to the city. I was sleeping soundly, but something happened to awaken me. The little men told me about it afterwards, but at the time I did not know what was going on.

All at once I gave a great sneeze. I woke up but did not know where I was. I was not on the ground where I had been. I was tied down, and even my left arm was not free now. I felt I was on something hard. Then I guessed they had put me on some kind of a wagon to get me to the city.

The wagon had been stopped to rest the horses. Little men had climbed over me, and some had even come up to my face. One of these men carried a spear, and he had put the spear into my nose, and I had made a great sneeze. At this the little men had all run in great fright, and I was awake.

Soon the hard thing I was tied down to began to move, and I was bumped along for the rest of the day. When it grew dark, the wagon stopped for the night. But there were camp-fires, and little men must have guarded me all the night. The wagon on which I lay was not as soft as the grass, but still I slept well.

Chapter III

I Am Given a House

As soon as it was light, the little horses were again hitched to the wagon and we started on towards the city. We got there about noon.

The wagon stopped before an old temple. It was the biggest building in the land. This temple was to be my home. There was a gate in the wall of the temple about four feet high, and about two feet wide.

There was a window on each side of the gate. And now the King's men began fastening chains through one of the windows and then around my left leg. Each chain was about six feet long. I could see that I was going to be able to move around a little.

The chains were about as big as the chains ladies wear around their necks in my country, but they put ninety of them around my leg; so all together, they were strong enough to hold me.

Across the road from this temple, there was a tower about five feet high. While the men were putting the chains on my legs, the King and Queen and all the lords had climbed to the top of this tower. From the tower, they could get a good look at me.

I was almost covered by the crowds of little people, who had come out from the city to see me. They brought ladders which they placed against me so they could climb up and walk around on my body. They looked into my ears and nose. They pulled at my buttons, and felt of my hair. I did not like to have all these little people running over me. But as I did not want to hurt them, I did nothing.

All at once they all left. I had heard some little horns blowing and some one calling out. It must have been one of the King's servants telling everyone to get down and go away because that is what they did.

By this time, the King's men had the ninety chains in place. They cut all the little strings that tied me down. I could once more stand upon my feet.

What a noise the people made when I stood up and lifted my arms above my head! And how they ran when I lifted my feet and took the few steps the chains would let me take. How good it felt to stand up and move!

I looked all around me as I stood

there. I could see far away over the countryside.

The countryside looked like our kitchen gardens. Their little fields were about as big as one of our flower beds. Their tallest trees seemed to be just a little taller than I was. Everything was fresh and green and pretty.

I could see the city on my left. The houses looked like the doll houses with which I had seen little girls playing.

Then I saw the King and his party coming down from the tower across the road.

A beautiful black horse was brought forward. The servants held his head and the King got on his back. I could see that the King was a fine rider, and it was well that he was. His horse had never seen anything like me and was afraid. The horse stood up on his back legs. But the King was not thrown off. I stood very still and soon the horse was more quiet. The little King rode over to me. His servants held the horse and he got down.

The King walked quite near me and stood looking up at me with a smile on his face. Then he waved his hand and called out some words. I saw that a line of servants were coming with more food for me.

The food had been put in wagons this time. The servants pushed the wagons near enough for me to reach them. As I was very, very hungry, I just picked up the little wagons and ate from them. Each wagon held enough to make me about three good bites. Ten wagons were full of meat and ten wagons were full of bread. They had brought wine in pails, each about as big as a thimble, and I drank all they had brought.

The Queen and the rest of the King's court had been carried across the road in chairs by the servants. They were sitting a little way from my feet, watching me eat. I could tell by the look on their faces, and the sound of their voices that they were very much surprised at how big I was, and how much I ate.

The little people were so small that when I was standing up, they hardly came to my shoe tops. I wanted to get a closer look at them. So I got down and lay on my side. My eyes were only three feet from the King. That way I could see him better.

The King was a very good-looking little man and was perhaps as much as one-half inch taller than any of the other men. He looked to be about twenty-eight years old.

The King was dressed in clothes that were fine, but not like the clothes people wore in my country. On his head was a little cap of gold, topped with a pretty little feather. In his hand, he held a sword with which he was ready to fight me if I should try to hurt any one. It was about three inches long.

The Queen and the rest of the King's party were dressed in very fine clothes. The King's clothes were rather plain while theirs were covered with flowers and birds worked in silver and gold.

All the while I was looking at the King, and he at me, the King kept talking to me. He had a high voice, and he spoke very clearly. But, of course, we could not understand each other.

There were two or three men in his court who were dressed differently from the others. These, I guessed, were teachers. They came quite near me and talked to me. I spoke to them in the different languages that I knew. But I could see by their faces that none of the words meant anything to them.

After about two hours, the King and his party went back to the palace but the soldiers stayed to watch me.

At first, I thought they were there to keep me from hurting any of their little countrymen. I soon found out that they were also there to keep their countrymen from hurting me.

When it got dark, I crawled into my house. I had to lie on the floor as there was no bed. But I took off my coat, used it for a pillow, and so spent my third night in this land of little people.

CHAPTER IV

I Learn the Language

I did not see the King for three weeks.

Many things were going on around my home. But since I could not understand the language, I could only guess at what was happening.

The very next morning, many little workmen came to my door, each carrying a pad a little bigger than he was. These they put on the floor and went away. Other workmen seated themselves on the floor and began to sew these little pads together. I could see that it was going to be a pad which I could use as a bed.

It took the workmen many days and much hard work to get it done. When at last it was spread on my floor, it was so thin that it did not make the floor seem much softer. I had seen other men sewing little pieces of cloth together and these turned out to be my sheets and blankets.

The soldiers were also busy outside my house. It seemed as though there were hundreds and hundreds of little people out there who wanted to see me. The soldiers had all they could do to keep them in order.

The little people could not climb around and over me now that I could move and stand up. The soldiers made them keep in line and out of my reach and moving.

Each day the King's servants brought me wagon loads of food and drink, so I was quite happy. I found that the King had ordered six hundred servants to take care of me. They came and put up tents outside my house.

Other men led or rode the King's horses by my house each day so that the horses would get used to me and not be afraid.

But the best thing of all was that the King sent six of his best teachers to teach me their language so that I could talk to the little people. And one of the first things I learned was that the country was called Lilliput. The little people called themselves Lilliputians. I learned very quickly to speak their language.

At the end of three weeks, the King came to see how things were going, and I could talk to him.

The first thing that I said to him was to thank him for the care his people had given me. Then I asked him to set me free, as I was tired of being chained to a wall.

The King shook his head and said that he could not do that just yet. He said he would talk it over with his lords. As soon as they all thought that it was safe, he would set me free. "Of course," he said, "you will first have to promise that you will never go to war against us." This I said I would gladly do.

The King said that they would be kind to me, and that if I would keep on doing as I had done, he thought the lords would soon set me free.

Then the King said, "It is the law of our land that anyone who comes here must let us see what is in his pockets."

I said, "I will do anything you

say. I will turn my pockets inside out if that is your wish!"

"You do not need to do that," he said. "I believe that you will not hurt my men. They will write down all the things that are in your pockets. Then I will ask you for the things which you might use to hurt us. Anything we take from you we will give back when you leave our country.

Part of this was said in words and part in signs, but the King understood me and I understood him. He went back to his palace and I waited for his men to come to look in my pockets.

The very next day, two soldiers came to my house and told me they had been sent by the King to see what was in my pockets. They had pen and paper which they put down on a little box.

When they were ready, I picked them

up very carefully and put them in one of my pockets. Then I held the top of the pocket open so that the light could get in, and they could see. When they had seen everything they called to me and I reached into my pocket and took them out. I put them down beside their box so they could write down what they had seen.

We did this with every pocket except one secret pocket which I did not show them. In this pocket, I kept my eye-glasses, a compass and a small telescope which I did not want to part with.

It must have looked very funny to see me putting these little fellows into a pocket, and taking them out again. They were very quiet about it, and would often talk together before they made up their minds just what to write.

When they were through, they thanked me and took their paper to the King.

Some weeks afterwards, the King told me what they had written down. He asked me in a very nice way to give him some of the things.

First, my sword. I took it out of my scabbard and held it up. When I did this, I heard a loud cry. I saw that all the King's soldiers were standing in back of him, with their bows and arrows ready to shoot me if I did not do as their King asked.

The King himself was not afraid. He asked me to put my sword back in the scabbard and put it on the ground as near him as I could reach. This I did.

He next asked me to take out my hollow iron post, by which he meant my pistol. Then he asked me what I could do with the hollow iron post. I told him I would fire the pistol. I did not put a bullet in it, but just some powder out of my bag. Then, telling

the King not to be afraid, I fired the
pistol into the air.

You never heard such a cry as went
up from the soldiers. Hundreds of
soldiers fell down as though they were
dead. They had never seen or heard
a pistol fired before. Even the King,
who was very brave, stood shaking for
a minute or two.

When the King and his soldiers found
out that they were not hurt, I put both
my pistols, my powder and bullets beside
the sword. I told the King that the
powder would go off if the smallest bit
of fire touched it. I asked that the
soldiers be very careful of it.

I also gave him my watch. The
King and my teachers had never seen
anything like the watch before. They
looked at it and felt it. They listened
to it. But they could not tell what it
was or what it was for. Then two

men came with a big post which they ran through the ring at the top of the watch. They then put the post on their shoulders and lifted the watch off the ground and carried it away.

I gave the King my money, my knife, my comb, my handkerchief, and the book I had in my pocket in which I put down what happened to me from day to day. These things he looked at and then gave back to me. The sword, pistol, bullets, and powder, and my watch were put in wagons and taken away.

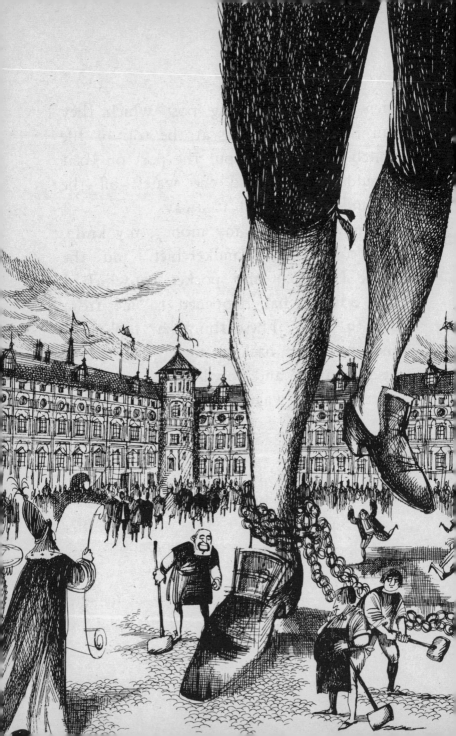

CHAPTER V

I Am Set Free

The thing I wanted most of all was to be set free. I was tired of being chained to that wall. I did everything I could to show the King and his people that I would not hurt them.

I do not think the King was ever afraid of me, for he was a very brave man. Soon I could see that some of the people were no longer afraid of me.

I would sometimes put down my hand and five or six of the little people would step up and stand on it. If I went to sleep lying on the ground, I would often find when I woke up that little boys and girls were playing in my hair. I was very careful not to move quickly at any time, or to move in such a way as to hurt or frighten them.

The horses of the soldiers were no longer afraid of me. They would come right up to my feet. I often held my hand down to the ground, and the soldiers would jump their horses over it. One soldier on a very fine horse once jumped his horse over my foot, shoe and all.

The King would often come and watch the soldiers. One day, he asked me to stand up and put my feet apart, and when I had done this, he marched all of his soldiers between my feet.

One day a messenger came to me and told me that the King and some of his men had been riding near the place where I had been found. There they saw a big, black thing lying on the ground.

The men thought it might be something that belonged to me. The King wanted to know if I would like to have it brought to me. I said I would, for I thought it might be my hat. I had not seen it since I came to the land of the Lilliputians.

In a few days, I heard a noise and down the road came something which I soon saw was my hat. The little men had made some holes in the edge of it through which they had run some ropes. The ropes were then tied to eight horses and they had pulled the hat down the road to me. The hat was dusty and, of course, had two holes in it, but still I was glad to get it.

Then one day, a man called Skyresh Bolgolam, and some of his friends came to see me. They had a big, long paper which Bolgolam himself had written and which he read to me.

It seemed that the King had talked to his court about setting me free. Everyone had been for it, except this one man, Skyresh Bolgolam. He was a very cross old man, and he did not like me. But he said he would be willing to set me free if I would promise some things.

These things he had written out himself and he read them to me. They were things that I promised to do, such as not going about the country unless the King said I could, keeping to the big roads, helping the King with the building of stone work, making a map of the country, and fighting for the King if he asked me to.

The paper was signed by the King, who had eight long names. I said I would be very glad to promise these things, and I signed my name.

As soon as I had done this, my chains were taken off and I was free.

The King and his court had come up

while Skyresh Bolgolam was reading the long paper to me. Bowing very low, I thanked them for setting me free.

The King answered and said he hoped I would be a friend of Lilliput.

I was now free and I could speak with the people of Lilliput. I began to learn all I could about them. I did not take many trips around the island because I felt it was very hard on these little people to have to stay in their houses whenever I wished to move about.

I was afraid that I would not see one of the Lilliputians. Then they might get under my feet and be stepped on and killed.

But I talked to everyone who came to serve me and since I could see a long way, I learned many things without leaving my house.

As I told you, my clothes did not

look very good after my long swim in the sea. The King of Lilliput had sent two hundred women to sew for me. Of course, they had no cloth in pieces big enough to make anything for me. And so they had to sew many pieces of their cloth together.

I lay down on the ground and the women measured me as best they could. I gave them my shirt and they measured it very carefully. In time, they made me a very nice, new shirt.

The King sent three hundred men to make me a new suit. This was a little harder to do. I got down on my knees, and they put ladders against me and dropped lines from my neck to the bottom of my coat. I helped them measure my arms, and my legs, and that was all they seemed to need. They soon made me a very nice suit. Though the little squares of cloth that they sewed together were all blue, they were not all the same color of blue. But the coat fit me very well.

I made myself a chair and a table out of the biggest trees they had in their forests. Now I did not have to sit on the floor any more to eat my food. But I did have to lift my servants and the dishes up onto the table.

My table top was very large and smooth, and the first time the King had come to see me after it was done, I had lifted up his coach, horses and all, and let him drive around on it. He had gone home and told his court about this. The next day two or three of the men from the King's court had driven out and asked me to let them drive around on my table. They had brought their wives and children, and from the way they laughed, I knew they thought it was great fun.

The wife of Flimnap, the man who took care of all the money, came three or four times, as she seemed to enjoy it very much. As her mother, her sister, and a friend or two were always with her, there was no reason for Flimnap to be angry about this but I found out later that he was.

One time the King asked if he and the Queen and their children could come and watch me eat. He wanted the children to learn more about me.

When they came, I lifted them up, along with the chairs their servants brought, and put them on my table. I lifted the soldiers who always came along to guard them, and placed them in back of the chairs of the King's family. Some of the King's court had come along also.   One of these was Flimnap.

Since the King and his family were watching me, I ate just as much as I could, and I could eat a lot of their food. The more I ate, the longer grew Flimnap's face. I could hear him talking to the King and I believe he was telling the King how much it cost each day to feed me.

When I stopped eating and the table had been cleared, the King asked that I lift his coach and horses up on the table so that he could take his family for a little ride. This I did.

Flimnap asked me to put him down on the floor. I took him between my fingers and put him down on the floor with great care. If I had known what trouble he was going to cause me, I think I would have squeezed him.

CHAPTER VI

I Visit the King's Palace

As soon as I was set free, I asked the King if I could visit the city. He said I could, but asked me again to be very sure that I did not hurt any of his people or their houses. The people were told what day I was coming so they could get off the streets.

The house in which I lived was outside the city wall. On the day on which I was to visit the city, I got ready and then walked along the road until I came to this wall.

The wall was about two and one-half feet high and wide enough so that a coach and horses could be driven along the top of it. Every ten feet or so, there was a strong tower in which soldiers stood with bows and arrows.

I stepped over this wall, being very careful where I put my feet. Once I was inside the wall, I was very careful not to knock a roof off or bump over a chimney. I had left my coat at home for the same reason, as its long tails could have taken all the shingles off their roofs. I soon saw that it could have taken off more than shingles, for every roof-top in town was covered with little people who wanted to get a good look at me.

I was so tall that I could get a good look at their whole city. It was built in a square, with two big wide streets which cut it into four parts. These streets were five feet wide and were the only ones I could walk in. They crossed in the middle of the square and there the King's palace stood. The smaller streets were only about one foot wide. The houses were all from three to five stories high and seemed to have many families.

I could see into their little stores and they seemed to be full of things to buy, though at this time their windows were full of little faces looking out to see my big feet going by.

The King's palaces stood inside a wall not quite as high as the city wall. There was room enough between the wall and the first palace for me to put one of my feet. But the palaces were about three feet tall and I could not step over them for fear of knocking off all the chimneys. The King and his family lived in the palace which was in the very center. The King had asked me to look into his windows so that I could see the Queen and his children in their fine home. This I could not do on this first visit. This time I saw the city, and the people saw me.

The next day, I went to one of their forests and cut down some trees with my knife. From these I made two stools each about three feet high and strong enough to hold me.

The next time I went to the city, I carried these stools in my hands. When I got to the palaces, I put one down between the wall and the first palace. I put the other stool on the other side of that palace. Then I stood on one stool and stepped right over the palace and on to the other stool. In this way I worked my way to the very center, to the palace where the King lived. Here there was room enough for me to step down, so I got down very carefully and looked into the windows of the King's home.

There I saw the Queen and her

children and her servants all looking
out at me. The Queen very kindly put
her hand out a window so that I could
kiss it.

I thanked the King and the Queen
for letting me visit their beautiful palace.
I then stepped up on my stools and
worked my way to the outer wall again.

Not long after that, one of the King's
men named Reldresal, came to see me.
He came in a coach pulled by two little
horses, and sent someone to my door
to ask me if I would talk to him. I
said I would be very happy to do so,
for I knew this little man well, and he
had always been very kind to me.

When he came in, I told him I would
be glad to lie down so he could talk
into my ear. But he said he would
rather I took him up in my hand so
that he could see my face as we talked.
This I did.

I began by thanking him for his help. He had been one of the men who had wanted to set me free.

Then Reldresal told me what he had come for. He began by saying,

"As you know, we do not always think alike about things in this country."

I told him it was the same in my country, and in every country I had visited. This was a surprise to him, but he went on. "We all fear that men from the Island of Blefuscu will come to try to take our island. You say there are other countries in which people like you live, but the only other country that we know about is Blefuscu. We have been fighting the people of Blefuscu since the time of our King's grandfather.

"It began this way. When our King's grandfather was a boy he started to eat an egg. He ate his egg in the way we always ate eggs, by breaking a hole in the big end and eating out the inside with his spoon.

"But he cut his finger on the eggshell. So his father, who was the King, at once made a law saying everyone should open the small end of their eggs and eat them from that end. This made some of our people very angry. They said they would go right on eating their eggs from the big end.

"The King sent his soldiers to fight with them, to make them eat their eggs from the small end. The people tried to fight the soldiers but there were too many soldiers and they had to stop fighting. But they did not give up.

"They went to the Island of Blefuscu whose King said they could eat their eggs in any way they liked. There were other wars when the people from the Island of Blefuscu came over to the Island of Lilliput.

"Many bad things happened just because some people would not eat their eggs from the small end. Books were written about it, and it is said that as many as eleven thousand people were killed because of it.

"The people who ate their eggs from the big end were called 'Big Endians.' They could not get work in Lilliput. More and more of them went to the Island of Blefuscu. The King of Blefuscu was glad to have them. At first, he sent his lords to talk to our King and tried to get him to change the law. He pointed out that the laws in the old, old books that we had always lived by said that one should break the egg at the end that was best. This could mean either the big or the little end of the egg.

"I think too, that this is right, but our King would not listen to the lords from the Island of Blefuscu and told his soldiers to make the people obey his new law.

"It made the King of Blefuscu angry when our King would not listen to his lords. There was much fighting and many have been killed. We have lost many big ships and as many as thirty thousand soldiers and seamen.

"But now the people of Blefuscu have built a lot of new ships, and it looks as if they were going to come again to the land of Lilliput. The King is afraid we cannot beat them without your help.

"Our King sent me to tell you these things and to ask you if you will help us fight the people of Blefuscu."

I thought about this for some time. Then I said, "The people of Lilliput have been good to me. So you may tell your King that I will do whatever I can to keep anyone from taking your country from you."

CHAPTER VII

I Help the King of Lilliput

I had never seen the Island of Blefuscu. It lay to the north of Lilliput and I had never gone to the north side of this country.

I talked to the sailors of Lilliput and found out all I could about the water between the Island Lilliput and the Island Blefuscu. They said in the deepest part, it was about seventy glum-guffs deep, which would be about six feet. They said that in most places it was not that deep.

Then one day I went north. When I was near the water, I looked carefully at the grass to be sure there were no little horses or cows, cats or dogs in it, and then lay down flat and crawled until I was close enough so that I could see the Island Blefuscu.

I took out my telescope, and with it, I could easily see the other island. It looked very much like Lilliput.

I could see about fifty fighting ships. I could see the little sailors on the ships. They also had many other ships which looked as though they were to be used to carry soldiers and their horses.

When I had seen all that there was to see, I came back to my house and sent word to the King that I had a plan. I thought I could win the war with Blefuscu without any fighting. I told him I would need a lot of their strongest rope and some bars of iron. The King was very glad to hear this and sent me what I asked for.

Since their strongest rope was only about as thick as a string, I twisted three ropes together to make one that was stronger. Their bars of iron were about as big as a knitting needle. I twisted two bars of iron together, and bent them so they had a hook at one end. I tied a long rope to the other end of the hook. Then I did the same with other bars of iron. When I had fifty of these I was ready to go to war.

I sent word to the King that I was ready to bring him the ships of Blefuscu.

He came himself to tell me that he and all of his court would come to the shore nearest Blefuscu that very next day to watch me. He wished me good luck and told me again and again how glad he was that I was going to help them.

The next morning I made ready to go. I had my telescope and my eyeglasses in my secret pocket. In my other pockets, I had a knife and a bottle of the medicine which they had rubbed on the places where the arrows had pricked my skin. I threw the little hooks on the ropes over my shoulder and carefully walked to the north shore.

When I got there, I took off my shoes and stockings, my coat and shirt, and quickly walked into the water. When the water got deep enough, I swam.

I could hear the cries of the lookouts on Blefuscu when they saw my big head coming through the water as I swam towards them. They had not seen me when I was still on the Island of Lilliput.

I have not words enough to tell you of what went on when I came near the shore where the water was not so deep. I stood up and began to walk towards their ships. Such a cry of fear went up from the sailors that the people in the city started running towards the water to see what was the matter.

The little sailors did not wait for the small boats to come and take them off the ships. They jumped into the water. The sea was black with them. They went swimming towards the shore where their friends pulled them out of the water.

As soon as I was close enough to the ships, I got to work. I went from ship to ship putting a little hook on each through a hole at the front. I was very careful to keep each one of the ropes in my hand.

Before I was through, the shores were black with little people and I knew the King and his soldiers had come. All of a sudden, I felt a rain of little arrows hit me. I knew the little arrows could not do anything to me except burn and sting unless they should hit my eyes. I stopped and put on my eye-glasses. I had brought them for just this reason. I worked as fast as I could, for the little arrows burned like fire, and I wanted to get out of their reach.

I soon had all the little hooks fast to the ships. I tied all the ropes together and began to pull. The ships did not move. I pulled harder. Still they did not move.

I went around behind the ships and saw that each one was fast to an anchor. So I took out my knife and cut the anchor ropes as quickly as I could. This let the ships move free.

Then I quickly pulled on the ropes that were fast to the hooks on the ships and walked away, pulling the ships after me.

Oh, what a cry went up from the Island of Blefuscu! I could see the King and his party. Some were crying, and some were just standing looking after me as though they could not believe their eyes. The soldiers were still shooting their little arrows at me but I was too far away now for them to hit me.

As soon as I was far enough away, I stopped and picked the little arrows out of my face and hands. The medicine I had brought soon stopped the pain, and I was all right again. I put my glasses back in my secret pocket, for I had not told the King about them, and I thought I might need them again.

I then walked and swam, pulling the ships toward the Island of Lilliput where I knew the King and his court were waiting.

The little men of Lilliput could begin to see the ships when I was about halfway. But since this was the deepest part of the water, and I was swimming, they could not see me. They thought that something had happened to me, and that the men of Blefuscu were coming to fight them.

When I came near the shore I saw the whole army of Lilliput drawn up on the shore. But as soon as they saw my head coming out of the water, they began to call out for joy.

When I was near the shore I held up the ropes to show the King how I was pulling the ships. And as I came to the shore I put the ropes down at his feet, crying, "Long live the King of Lilliput!"

The King was very, very happy. After he had thanked me, he held up his hands and all the people who had come to watch became quiet. "To thank the Man Mountain for what he had done this day, I now make him a Nardac!"

To be a Nardac is the highest honor one can get in Lilliput. I was very happy, for I had helped the people of Lilliput who had been so good to me.

The little people were so thick around there that I could not come out of the water without stepping on some of them. I had to wait until they had all gone to their homes. Then I carefully walked to my house.

The hundreds of little men and women who cooked for me were ready with my food. I sat and ate wagon load after wagon load of good food. I could not help feeling sorry for the King of Blefuscu who had lost all his beautiful little ships.

But I was glad that the war was over and that not one of the little men on either island had been killed.

CHAPTER VIII

I Learn the King's Plans

The very next day the King sent me a letter which made me very sad. It showed that while in most ways he was a very wise King, still in other ways he was as foolish as his grandfather, who went to war because of the way people ate eggs.

The King, in his letter, asked me to return to Blefuscu and bring back all the rest of their ships. He then would move in with his soldiers and make the people of Blefuscu his slaves.

I went to the King and tried to get him to see that this was very wrong. But he would not change his mind. And so I had to tell him that I would not do as he wished. I told him that I did not think it was right to make slaves of free, brave people, and that I would not help him do it.

The King was very angry but he acted in a friendly way and thanked me for coming. But from that time on, he was not my friend.

Soon the King of Blefuscu sent some of his highest lords to ask the King of Lilliput for peace. Without my help, the King of Lilliput knew he could not win a war with them even if he did have most of their ships. So he said he, too, wanted peace.

Before these men went back to Blefuscu, they came to my house to talk to me. They had heard that I would not help the King of Lilliput make the people of Blefuscu his slaves. They spoke a different language than the Lilliputians. I could not understand them. But many of the Lilliputians could speak the language of Blefuscu, so the Lilliputians told me what the men from Blefuscu said.

They thanked me for not helping the king of Lilliput in his wish to make them slaves. They said that the King of Blefuscu wanted very much to see me.

I said I would like to visit their country before I went to my own home. So, in the name of their King, they asked me to visit their country. I said I would be very glad to do so if it pleased the King of Lilliput, whom I had promised to obey. They then went back to their island.

When I went to the King of Lilliput and asked him if I could go to the Island of Blefuscu to visit that King, he said I could, but he did not smile or seem a bit friendly.

One night, one of my servants came to me and said there was a man at my door who wished to see me. He said this

man was my friend but he did not wish
to be seen by anyone who would tell
the King he had visited me.

I went to my door, and though it
was very dark, I could see there a little
carrying-chair with its curtains drawn.
I picked up the chair and very carefully
put it in my pocket.

Then I told all my servants that I
wanted to be alone, and when they had
all gone, I closed the door to my house
and lighted a candle. Then I took the
little chair out of my pocket, and set
it on my table close to the candle and
said, "Now we are alone. Will you
please come out?"

The little curtains were pulled back
and out stepped one of the men from
the King's court. I will not give his
name for I do not want him to get
into trouble, as he is one of my best
friends.

I could see that he was very sad and also very much afraid. He seemed to be in a hurry and he talked very fast.

"My friend," he said, "you are in great danger and I have come to tell you. If the King ever finds out that I have been here I will be killed."

Then he went on to tell me of the plans that the King and Flimnap had made to kill me. My friends in the court had begged for my life, and so the King had said that he would let me live. But because I had not helped the King make slaves of the people of Blefuscu, my eyes were to be put out. All this was to happen in three days.

I thanked my brave little friend and carefully put him outside in his chair. Two of his servants who were hiding in the darkness came up and carried his chair away. I went inside my house to think about what he had told me.

I sat in my house and thought for a long time. Before morning came, I knew what I must do.

The King had already told me I could go to visit the Island of Blefuscu. Because he did not know that I knew what plans he had made for me, he would think nothing of it if I went to make my visit. I would go to the Island of Blefuscu and not come back.

That very morning, I sent word to the King that I was going to the Island Blefuscu and I did not wait for an answer. My servants went out to tell everyone to keep off the roads, and when I thought it was safe, I set out.

I took with me only the things I had in my pockets and my blanket. I went north to the side of the island nearest Blefuscu. I took off my shoes and stockings and my coat and put them and my blanket on one of the empty

ships that I found there, so they would
stay dry. Then, taking hold of the ship's
anchor rope, I pulled it after me and
walked out into the water and left the
Island of Lilliput.

CHAPTER IX

I Visit Blefuscu

The people of Blefuscu saw me coming when I walked out of the water on to their island. There were some men waiting to show me the way to the King's palace. As these men spoke the language the people of Lilliput used, I could understand them.

I put on my dry clothes and combed my hair. Then I took two of the little men up in my hands and put them near my ear. They told me which way to go.

When we were close to the palace, I heard the little men in my hands calling, "Stop! Stop here! Wait here for the King!"

I stopped and stood very still. I put my coat to rights and made myself look as nice as I could. I waited for the King.

After an hour the gates to the palace yard were opened and out came the King and all his court. The Queen and her ladies came next in their chairs, carried by their servants. No one seemed to be at all afraid of me now.

The King and the ladies came near to me. I got down on my hands and knees and put my head very close to the ground and kissed the hands of the King and Queen.

I told them that I was very happy that the King had asked me to visit his country. I said that if there was anything he would like to have me do that would not hurt my own King, the King of Lilliput, I would be glad to do it.

Of course, I said these things in the words I had learned in Lilliput. I did not tell him that the King of Lilliput was no longer my friend.

I will not tell you of all the kind things the King of Blefuscu did for me. He could not have done more for another king. The only thing he could not give me was a house big enough for me to sleep in and so I had to sleep on the sand by the sea. But I covered myself with the blanket which I had brought with me.

Three days after I came to Blefuscu, I saw something out in the sea. It was very big, and looked like a boat which had been turned upside down. I watched it as the wind and the waves brought it near to the land. It was a boat from a ship such as the one I had been on. It must have been washed away in a storm.

I could not get the boat, so I went back and asked the King for help. I asked him to let me have twenty of the

best ships he had and three thousand
sailors to help me bring in the boat.
He said he would be glad to help me.
The ships were made ready and sailed
out towards the boat.

I took off my clothes and walked out
as far as I could go. Then I swam to
the boat. The sailors followed me. They
threw me their strongest ropes and I tied
many of them together and tied them to
the boat. Then I gave the ropes to each
of the ships. The sailors made the ropes
fast to the ships and then they set sail
towards the land. They pulled and I
swam behind the boat and pushed it as
hard as I could.

We did not move the boat very fast,
but at last we got it near enough so that
I could push it up on the sand. It was
still upside down and I was not strong
enough to turn it over. But I was glad

I had it up on the sand where it could not go out to sea again.

The boat was a very big one, big enough to hold eight or ten men my size. I knew that if I could get it turned over and fitted with a sail, I could sail away from these islands.

The first thing to do was to get it turned over. To do this I would need a large pole, and much help. I had to cut down some of their biggest trees and tie them together to get a pole big enough to use. I tied many of their little ropes together to get a rope strong enough to pull with. At last I got everything together.

The King sent me three hundred horses with men to lead them. We tied ropes to them and then to the boat. Then when I called "go," the little horses pulled and I put my big pole under the boat and pushed. The boat turned over on the sand.

I was very happy to see that the boat had no holes in it. There were no oars. The only thing I had to cut with was my pocket knife, but I made a pretty good pair of oars.

By digging the sand away from around the boat, I got it to float on the water.

When I tried to row the boat, I found that it was big and heavy, but that I could move it. I rowed it around the island and into their ship yards to work on it. Then I went to the King who, of course, knew all about my find. I told him that I would like to fit my boat with some sails because I would like to leave and try to get back to my own country.

When I told the King this, he said he would like to talk to me about some other things. I found a place where I

could sit down without hurting anything, lifted the King and his guards onto
a roof near my face, and we had a
long talk.

The King of Blefuscu said he would
be very happy if I would stay on their
Island and help them, and never go back
to Lilliput. I thanked him but said I
would like very much to go back to my
own country.

When the King heard me say I did
not wish to stay, he said, "Then I think
it would be well for you to leave as
soon as you can. The King of Lilliput
may hear of your plans and he will be
very angry. I will give you all the help
you need to make your boat ready to
go to sea."

The next morning, five hundred workmen came to help me. I put them to
making sails. Their sail cloth was as
thin as my handkerchief, so I had them

sew twelve layers of sail cloth together before they cut the sails. That made it so heavy that they could hardly lift it but it made sails strong enough to sail my boat.

I used the pole I had made to turn my boat over, to put the sail on, and I myself made the ropes I needed. I tied twenty of their little ropes together to make one strong enough to use on my sail.

I worked as fast as I could to get ready to go. I wanted to take some of these little animals home to show my people. The King gave me some. I made a place in my boat for six of their best cows and sheep. I took hay and corn and water for them.

I would have liked very much to take some people, but the King would not let me. He made me promise not to take any of them even if they wanted to go.

Just to make sure that none of his people left Blefuscu, he had some of his men look through my pockets before I left.

The day before I left, there was a long line of servants coming and going all day. They were carrying food to my boat. I did not know how long it would take me to find a ship which would take me home and so I took all the food I could carry.

That evening I went to the King's palace and asked to see him. The King and his whole family came out to tell me goodbye.

I told them goodbye, and said that I would sleep on the sand near my boat. Then before it was light the next morning, I would set sail in my boat. Again, I thanked the King and all the people of Blefuscu for all the help they had given me.

CHAPTER X

I Get Home Again

The next morning I was up before it was light. I ate the food which had been left on the shore for me. I then stepped into my boat and set my sails. As early as it was, there were many of the little people on the shore to see me go.

When the wind filled my sails and my boat began to move over the water, a loud cry went up from the shore. The little people were calling their word which meant goodbye.

I waved to them and took one last look at their little island. Then I took my pocket compass from my secret pocket and sailed my boat to the north.

I sailed northward for three days. Just as my food and water were about gone,

I saw a sail far, far away upon the edge of the sea.

I sailed towards it as fast as I could, and I could see that I was getting nearer, for the sail seemed larger.

As soon as I was near the ship, I called out as loudly as I could. For a while, no one seemed to hear me. But soon I saw a flag sent up and so I knew they had seen me.

They then took down their sails and came to a stop, and in half an hour, I came up to the side of the ship.

I cannot tell you how happy I was to see that the flag they were carrying was the flag of my own country. They put down a rope ladder to me. I carefully put my cows and sheep into my pockets and climbed on board.

The first face I saw as I came on board was that of an old friend, Peter Williams, who had once sailed on a ship with me. I was so glad to see someone I knew. He took me straight to the Captain and told him who I was and all that he knew about me.

The Captain asked me where I had come from, and why I had been sailing alone out on the sea in such a small boat.

When I told him my story, the Captain looked at me in a very queer way and I knew he thought I had lost my mind. But I soon was able to show him that I had not.

I took some of his books and laid them in a square in an open place on his desk to make a fence. Then I reached into my pockets and took out my little cows and sheep and placed them inside the square. They began to run around and to moo and baa as loud as they could. Then he knew I had been telling the truth.

The sailors made me very welcome on

board. They helped me fix a place on the deck for my little cows and sheep, which they never got tired of watching.

We got to England in April, seven months after I had left Blefuscu.

I was very happy to see my family again. My boy John was a big boy in school now, and my little girl Betty was nearly grown up. An uncle had died and left me a lot of money, and my father had left me an inn that paid well. So my family were well taken care of.

I went to sea again after a few years, but I never again saw the Island of Lilliput.

PART II

My Voyage
to
Brobdingnag

I Come
to a Strange Country

I had only been home in England about two months when I again went to sea. I loved the sea and I could not be happy on land. I signed on as a ship's doctor and we sailed away towards the Cape of Good Hope.

We were a long, long way from home when a very bad storm came up and we were blown far off our course. We did not see any land for days and days. We had enough food to eat, but our drinking water was nearly gone.

Then one day, the look-out saw land on our right. We sailed as near to it as our ship could go. Then the sailors lowered a small boat and filled it with empty water barrels. The Captain called out a dozen men, and told them to row to shore and fill the barrels with water.

I asked the Captain if I might go along so that I could see the country.

When we came to the land, we saw no one around. But we found a spring of fresh water. The men began to fill their water barrels. I walked away to see what kind of land it was. The country was very bare and rocky. At last I turned and started back towards the place where I had left the men.

When I came to a place where I could see the ship, what did I see but the men already in the small boat, rowing towards the ship as fast as they could! I opened my mouth to call to them. But before I could cry out, I saw something else!

Behind them, and chasing them was a giant. He was as tall as a big tree in my country. He was walking in the water, which did not come much higher than his knees.

I did not wait to see whether the giant caught the men or not. I just turned and ran as fast as I could go!

I ran and ran among the rocks until I came to some very high grass. It was twenty feet high. I made my way through it and came to what seemed to me was a big wide road.

I walked down this road for a long way. I could not see much except the very high grass and some tall plants that looked like wheat except that they were forty feet high. Then I came to a hedge which I could see ran along the side of the field. It was made of bushes that were about one hundred feet high.

There were some steps built so that any one could climb over this hedge and into the next field. But each step was six feet high and I could not climb them.

I was trying to squeeze through between the bushes of the hedge when I saw something through the leaves. One of those giants was coming towards me.

He looked even bigger than the man I had seen running after my friends in the boat. I turned and ran back into the wheat field.

Then I heard an awful noise. It sounded like thunder but I knew at once that it was the voice of the giant. I looked up and saw him standing on top of the steps with his hands to his mouth, calling to someone. Very quickly, seven other men, all as big as he, but not dressed quite so nicely, came out of the field behind him. Each one carried a very big knife!

He spoke to them in words I could not understand. Then they began to cut down the wheat in which I was hiding.

I moved ahead of them as fast as I

could. Soon I came to a part of the field where the wheat had been blown down and I could go no farther. I could hear them close behind me. I was very much afraid, but I could not get through the wheat.

I could not help thinking of Lilliput. There I must have seemed as big to the Lilliputians as these men seemed to me.

I wondered if the big men were kind, or whether they were as bad as they were big. Then one of the men was almost upon me.

I was afraid one of his big feet would step on me, or that his big knife would cut me in two before he saw me. So I stepped out into an open space. I screamed as loudly as I could!

The giant looked down and saw me on the ground. For a while, he just looked at me the way I have looked at a little animal and watched it to see what it would do. Then he reached down and took me between his fingers. He lifted me up to his face.

He held me so tightly that he hurt me. I was wise enough not to kick or fight for if I had done so he might have dropped me and I would have been killed.

He was holding me so tight and hurting me so much that I could not help crying. When he saw the tears running down my face, he must have guessed that he was hurting me. He ran to his Master, who was the man I had first seen.

The Master listened as the servant talked. Then he looked at me for a long time. He lifted my coat as though he wanted to see what was under it. After he had looked me all over, he called the others to come and see me.

Then he picked me up very gently and put me on the ground on my hands and knees. I got to my feet at once and walked around. They all got down on the ground so that they could see me better. I took off my hat and bowed to them. I talked to them even though I knew they could not understand me.

Then the farmer talked to me. His voice was so loud it hurt my ears. After a little while, the farmer sent his men back to work. Then he took his handkerchief out of his pocket and spread it on his hand. He put his hand on the ground and made me a sign to step on to it. It was only about a foot high, so I did. I was afraid I would fall off if he moved his hand, so I lay down. He carried me to his house.

When we got to the house, he called his wife, and showed her what was in his handkerchief. She screamed as my wife does when she sees a mouse. But she soon got used to me.

Since it was dinner time, the farmer put me down in the middle of a big table and the family sat down to eat.

There was a large dish of meat on the table. The farmer's wife took one of her small plates, cut some bread and meat into small pieces and gave it to me. I thanked her, then took my knife and fork out of my pocket and began to eat.

I had to stand up to eat. This seemed very funny to them. They all laughed very loudly. The wife then sent for a glass that was much smaller than the ones they were using.

This glass was so heavy that I had to take both hands to lift it to my mouth. Before I drank, I bowed to the farmer's wife the way we do in England. This, too, must have been very funny to the giants. They all laughed so loudly it made my ears ring again.

The drink was very good. It tasted

like the cider we had at home. I could not drink it all and I could not eat all the bread and meat which the farmer's wife had given to me. But I must say I enjoyed my first meal in this strange country.

CHAPTER II

I Have Some Bad Times

After we had finished eating, the farmer made a sign that told me he wanted me to come to his end of the table.

As I walked toward him, his little boy, who was sitting beside him, reached out and picked me up. He took hold of me by one foot and held me way up in the air above the table the way I had seen little boys hold a kitten. I was so frightened I cried out, but the farmer moved very quickly to save me. He put his hand under me and hit the boy so hard that he let go of me and I dropped safely into the farmer's hand.

He put me down on the table, and would have sent the boy to his room.

But I laughed and acted as though I thought it was just a boyish thing to do. I tried to make the farmer let the boy off, because I wanted the boy to like me. The farmer seemed to understand for he let the boy come back to the table.

Just then the cat jumped into the lap of the farmer's wife, and began to purr. I heard this awful roaring noise and turned and looked into the face of the gigantic animal. It frightened me so that I wanted to run and hide though I was forty feet away from her. She was about three times as big as a cow and could have eaten me in one bite!

The wife was holding her very tightly as if she, too, was afraid the cat would jump at me. The farmer picked me up and put me down right in front of the cat to see what she would do, but she did not even look at me.

This made me feel very brave, so I walked back and forth in front of the cat, three or four times and she drew back as though she were afraid of me, which made me feel better.

There were three or four dogs in the room also, each one about as big as an elephant. But I was not as afraid of them as I was of the cat.

Dinner was over and the farmer got ready to go back to his work. He talked to his wife and I guessed that he was telling her to take good care of me. I was so tired that I tried to show her that I wanted to sleep, and she understood me. She took me into another room in which there was a very large bed. She put me down in the middle of it, covered me with a handkerchief as large as the biggest sail on our ship and left me there to rest.

I had been sleeping for about two

hours, and I was dreaming about my wife and children, when I woke up in this big room on this big, big bed.

I walked to the edge of the bed and looked over. I could see no way of getting down to the floor. The bed was sixty feet off the floor.

The farmer's wife had gone away. I knew I could not call loud enough for her to hear me, as the kitchen was very far away, and the door was shut.

I had just made up my mind to lie down again and rest, when I heard a noise in the curtain. I looked and there were two rats running up the curtains. They were as big as the biggest of dogs, and I could see that they were expecting to eat me!

The rats jumped off the curtains and on to the bed. They came towards me as fast as they could run.

I drew out my sword and got ready

to fight though I was very much afraid that the two of them would be too much for me.

But I was lucky. One of them jumped at me and put his front feet on my collar and I ran my sword into his heart before he could hurt me and he fell back dead.

The other turned to run when he saw what happened to the first one. I ran over the bed after him, and I hurt him with my sword quite badly before he got away.

Soon after this, the farmer's wife came in and cried out in surprise when she saw the signs of the fight which I had been through. She took me up in her hand to see if I was hurt. I smiled and showed her that I was all right.

CHAPTER III

I Get a Nursemaid
and Friend

When we were at the table, I had seen the farmer's daughter. She had smiled at me very kindly. Though she was very big, I could see that she was just a young girl. Later I learned that she was only nine years old.

Her mother called her in now and I could guess from the way they acted that the mother was giving me into the daughter's care. From that day on, as long as I was in the country, this little girl was my nursemaid, teacher and friend.

That first day, they fixed me a bed where I would be safe from the rats. They brought out what seemed like a very big bed to me, but which I could tell was the girl's baby bed. This they made up for me and placed on a hanging shelf so that no rats could get at me. When night came, my nursemaid picked me up and put me in this high place. I felt very safe.

The very next day, my nurse began to teach me to speak their language. She would do this by pointing her finger at something and saying its name. Then I would say it after her. Soon I could ask for things I wanted. She called me "Grildrig" which means something like "little man." I called her "Glum-dal-clitch" which means "little nurse."

She could sew very well for so young a girl and she began to make me some clothes. She made them of the finest cloth she could get, but which was like the cloth with which we make grain bags in our country. The clothes fit me very well. She made me seven shirts and other clothes in the days that followed.

She was very good to me and did everything she could to make me happy. At first, she seemed to think I was more like a doll-baby than a man. But after I could speak her language, we got along very well together. One of the things she told me was that the name of her country was Brobdingnag.

Very soon, it began to be known all around the country that my Master had found a funny little man in his wheat field. Everyone wanted to see me.

The first one to come was an old farmer who lived nearby. He was a friend of my Master. My Master brought me out and put me on the empty dinner table.

I walked up and down in front of the old man, with my sword in my hand. I bowed to him and asked him in his own language how he was, just as my little nurse told me to do.

He could not see very well, so he took out some glasses and put them on his nose. Then he put his face very close to me and looked at me. He looked so funny that I had to laugh. When my little nurse asked me why I was laughing, I told her his eyes looked like two moons outside a glass window. This made everyone laugh. But it made the old man very angry.

After this old man had looked at me, he took my Master off in a corner and talked to him a long time. From the way they acted and looked at me, I had a feeling that they were making plans for me.

The next morning, I found out this was true. My little nurse was crying when she came to take me down from my high bed. She held me close to her as though I were a dear doll, and from her I heard the whole story.

She had heard her mother and father talking after the old man had gone home. The old man had told her father he could make a lot of money by taking me to town on market day and making people pay money to see me. She told me that her father was going to take me to market.

My little nurse was crying because she was afraid someone would take me up in their hands and hurt me. She was afraid, too, that my feelings would be hurt if I had to show myself before all kinds of people. And she was also crying because she felt that her mother and father had not been kind to her. She told me that one year they had given her a pet lamb and said it would always be hers. But later her father had sold the lamb.

I tried to make her feel better by telling her that I did not mind too much. I felt that had the King of England been in my shoes, they would have done the same with him.

The very next day, my Master took me to town. He fixed up a box to carry me in. And he let my little nurse ride behind him on his big horse and carry me in the box. She had lined the box with a bed quilt. But even so, it was a bad trip for me. The horse took steps forty feet long. With each step, my box went up and down like a ship in a great storm. It took only thirty minutes to get to town, but I was very badly shaken up.

My Master stopped at an Inn where he was known. He rented a room for the day. Then he sent out a servant to tell everyone about me.

I could hear the servant out in the street telling everyone that they should come to the Inn and see the queer little animal that was to be seen there. He said I was not as big as a splaenuck (an animal which was six feet long) but that I looked just like a man. He said I could talk and could do one hundred tricks.

I was placed on a table in the largest room of the Inn which must have been three hundred feet square. My little nurse sat beside the table to take care of me and to tell me what to do.

My Master would let only thirty people into the room at one time.

I walked around on the table, turning around so that they could see me from all sides. I took out my sword and waved it around. I bowed to them. My nurse asked me questions which she knew I could answer and I answered them as loudly as I could.

I took up a thimble which I used as

a cup and drank from it after wishing them all good health.

I was shown to twelve sets of people that day. My Master would let no one touch me except my nurse. He made the people sit back from the table so that no one could reach me.

One school boy did throw a nut at me which only missed me by an inch or two. It would surely have killed me if it had hit me, for it was very hard and as large as a pumpkin. My Master gave him a good beating and threw him out of the room, but it frightened me very badly. Before night came, I was so tired that I could hardly lift my sword.

My Master told everyone that he would bring me again next market day and we went home, but I was so tired that for three days I could hardly stand up, and could not speak a word. However, I did not get as much rest as I needed, for the farmer's friends began to come to his house to see me. Nearly every day there would be thirty or more of these great giants coming to see me. The only day I really could rest was Wednesday, which was their Sunday, and everybody rested on Wednesday.

My Master made a lot of money showing me. But he thought he could make more if he took me to the big city. So he got some one to run his farm and told his wife goodbye. My Master and I and my little nurse rode away on his big horse one morning. It was August 17th, 1703, just two months after I had come to that country.

CHAPTER IV

I Am Taken to the Queen

My Master, who was really a kind man, had listened to the words of a neighbor who thought only of making money. Now my Master was going to take me to the biggest city in Brobdingnag to show me to the people, and make as much money as he could.

The city was three thousand miles away. I rode in a box tied to the waist of my little nursemaid as she sat behind her father on a horse. My nursemaid had put a quilt all over the inside of the box, with a bed in it for me. But it was a hard journey.

My little nursemaid tried to help. She would take me out as often as she could and hold me in her hand so I could see the country.

We were on the road for ten weeks. My Master stopped at all the big towns to show me.

When we came to the big city, my Master got a room on a busy street not far from the palace of the King and the Queen. Then he got a big table to put me on and began to let people in to see me. I was shown ten times each day.

I could speak their language quite well now and could understand what they said to me. I talked to the people which pleased and surprised them very much. More and more of them came to see me. But it seemed as though the more money my Master made, the more he wanted.

This was too much for me. I was tired all the time, and I became very thin. I couldn't eat. Soon I looked so bad my Master thought I was going to die.

About this time, the Queen sent a messenger to my Master asking him to take me to the palace so that she might see me. Some of her ladies had seen me.

My Master and his daughter, my nurse, took me to the palace that very day.

We were shown into the room where the Queen and her ladies were seated. My nurse took me out of my box and put me on a table close to the Queen. My Master and my nurse bowed very low.

I, too, bowed very low before the Queen, and said, "May I kiss your hand, your Majesty?"

The Queen was very much surprised to hear me speak in their language. She held out her hand to me. It was so big that I could not kiss the back of it as I would have done in my country. I put both my arms around the littlest finger and kissed the end of it.

The Queen asked me questions about my own country, and about how I had come to Brobdingnag.

Then she said, "Would you like to live here at the palace?"

I said, "Your Majesty, if I could do as I wish, I would be very happy to live here and serve you. But I belong to the farmer and I do not think he will let me go."

The Queen turned to the farmer and said, "Will you sell me this little man for one thousand pieces of gold?"

This pleased the farmer very much. He thought I was going to die anyway, and so he said, "Yes, yes, your Majesty!"

The Queen sent for the money and gave it to him at once.

Before he and my nurse could leave, I spoke to the Queen.

"Your Majesty," I said, "let me keep my nurse. She has been so kind to me.

She knows just how to take care of me. Please let her stay here, also."

This pleased the farmer. He thought all his neighbors would look up to him if his daughter lived in the King's palace. My little nurse could not keep back the tears of joy. The Queen said Glum-dal-clitch could stay. She told her father goodbye, and he left.

After he had gone, the Queen asked me if he had been good to me and I told her he had not. I showed her how thin I was.

I then added, "But now that I belong to your Majesty, I know I will be taken care of. I am sure I will soon be as strong as ever."

Then the Queen took me up in her hand and said, "I must show you to the King." I lay down in her hand so that I would not fall.

When she showed me to the King,

he gave me a very cold look. He could not see me very well, and he thought I was a small animal, something like a mouse, which they call a splaenuck.

He said to the Queen, "Why are you playing with a splaenuck?" This made the Queen smile, but she did not say anything. She just picked me up with her other hand and stood me on the table.

"Now," she said to me, "tell the King all about yourself."

So I told the King how I had come to his Brobdingnag. My nurse, who had followed the Queen, told them that all I said was true.

The King was very much surprised. But he did not believe my story. At first, he thought I was a toy that run by clockwork. But when he heard me speak and answer questions, he knew that could not be true.

The King sent for three of his wisest

men and had them look me over. They asked me many questions.

Then they told the King, "We do not know what he is. By the looks of his teeth, we know he eats meat. But he is not big enough to kill the smallest mouse. We do not see how he can keep himself alive.

"He cannot fly or dig holes in the earth, or climb trees like a squirrel. We do not know how he keeps away from animals that might eat him."

After they had looked me all over again, they made up a name for me that meant a "nothing."

I told them I came from a country where there were many millions like me, both men and women. I told them that our animals, trees, and houses were all the right size for us. I told them that we could easily make a living and take care of ourselves. They just smiled.

The King then sent for the farmer, who had not left town. He asked the farmer many questions. When the farmer told the same story that I had told, the King began to think it might be true. He gave orders that my nurse and I were to have the best of care.

We were given a room all to ourselves and four servants to take care of us. The Queen's own carpenter began to make me a much better box to live in.

It was very much like a bedroom, sixteen feet square and twelve feet high. It had windows and doors.

The board that made the ceiling was made so that it could be lifted off. They made me a nice bed which my nurse took out and aired every day. The Queen bought the finest silk she could find and had clothes made for me. The silk was as thick as a blanket but it made better clothes than those I had.

A man who made doll furniture made me some little chairs and a table and a set of silver dishes.

The Queen liked me very much. I ate all my meals at her table. My table and chair were lifted up and put on her table beside her plate.

The Queen, who did not eat nearly as much as most people in Brobdingnag, would take as much in one bite as twelve hungry English farmers could eat for a meal. What she thought was a small bit of bread would be the size of two of our biggest loaves. She drank out of a golden cup that held more than our biggest barrels.

On Wednesdays, the King and Queen and all their children ate together. Then the King would talk to me very kindly.

My life in the palace of the King and Queen of Brobdingnag was very happy.

CHAPTER V

My Life in the Palace

I lived very happily in the palace of the King and Queen of Brobdingnag for a long time. Of course, things happened to me which frightened me, but it was only because I was so small in this big, big land.

One time, my nurse took me outside for a walk. There was a storm coming up. She left me alone for a few minutes. While she was gone, the wind began to blow and before she could get back to me, large hail stones began to fall. They were as big as apples and hard as rocks. The first one that hit me knocked me to the ground. Each hailstone that fell on me hurt me very badly. I crawled towards a bush on my hands and knees with these big hail stones hitting my back so hard I thought they would break my bones.

I cried for help as loudly as I could. My nurse came quickly and found me hiding under the bush. She put me into my box and ran into the palace. I was so black and blue that I had to stay in my bed for ten days.

Another time, when we were in the garden, a dog who belonged to one of the workmen quietly picked me up in his mouth and carried me to his Master. I was surprised and frightened. As he was a hunting dog and used to carrying birds in his mouth, he did not hurt me at all. The workman, who was a friend of mine, felt very badly when he saw what his dog had done.

He picked me up in his hand and asked me if I was all right. When I told him that I was all right he took me back to my nurse. We never told the Queen about it for fear she would be angry at the dog or the workman and the Queen might not let us go into the garden again.

Once a large bird which was hunting for food nearly caught us. He must have thought I was a mouse because he flew down and just missed me by a foot or two. I drew my sword and ran for a tree. I thought I would hide from him if I could, and fight for my life if I had to. But the bird went away.

Another time I fell into a hole some animal had made. I got out of the hole by myself, but I told no one. I felt it was a little foolish for a man to get into that kind of trouble.

Another thing that made me feel foolish was the way the birds acted when they were around me. They were not afraid of me at all but would come right up to me while looking for food. If I tried to drive them away with a stick they would turn and pick at me with their sharp bills. Since the smallest of these birds was bigger than one of our turkeys you can be sure I was careful not to let one get very near to me.

The other things I did not like were the flies and wasps. There were many flies in this country in the summer. Each fly was as big as one of our crows. You can see why I did not want them lighting on me or on my food. I used to fight them with my sword, which always made the Queen laugh.

One sunny morning my nurse put my box on a window sill. I opened my window as I sat there eating a piece of cake. All at once, about twenty wasps flew in. One took a piece of my cake and flew out the window with it. Others flew around my head, making a loud noise that frightened me very much.

I drew my sword and killed four of them, and the rest flew away. I cut up the four that I killed and took out their stingers which were an inch and a half long, and sharp as needles. I saved these very carefully and later took them back to England with me.

All the people in the palace were very kind to me except the Queen's dwarf. Before I came, he had been the Queen's pet, so I could see why he did not like me. I tried as hard as I could to be kind to him and to stay out of his way. He was always trying to hurt me if he could, or make me look foolish.

At one time, when my nurse and I were walking in the garden, he hid behind an apple tree. As we walked under it, he shook the tree and apples as big as barrels fell on us. Of course, they did not hurt my nurse, but the one that hit me knocked me flat. My nurse put her hand over me and kept any more from falling on me, so I was not hurt very much.

Another time, we were at the table and the Queen had just picked the meat off a large hollow bone. She turned her head to speak to one of her ladies and while she was not looking, the dwarf picked me up and pushed me into that hollow bone clear up to my waist.

I did not want to cry out, so I just had to stay there until my nurse saw me. I was not hurt, but the Queen was very angry. She was going to have the dwarf beaten but I asked her not to. The dwarf knew I had saved him from a beating, but he still did not like me.

Then one day, he went too far. That day my nurse had gone to the other end of the table for something. The dwarf climbed up on a chair. He reached over and took me around the middle and dropped me into the Queen's cream pitcher.

The Queen threw up her hands and cried out. But she could not think what to do to save me. It was well for me that I was a good swimmer for it was a little while before my nurse could get there and find out what the trouble was.

When she saw what had happened, she quickly took a spoon and got me out. Then she took me to my box and brought warm water so I could wash the cream off myself. The Queen was very, very angry at the dwarf.

This time he was given a good beating and even made to drink the cream I had been dropped into. Soon after that the Queen gave him away and I never saw him again.

CHAPTER VI

My Traveling Box

I wished very much to see more of this big country. My nurse tried to take me with her one day when she was going for a ride in one of the Queen's carriages. She held my box on her lap but it was a little too large for her to hold very well. And we soon found that it was not safe for me.

The furniture moved over the floor. When the wheels of the carriage dropped into a hole in the street, my nurse only felt a little bump. But since the holes were about forty feet deep, I felt a big bump. My chairs and tables went flying around the room and nearly hit me.

I called to my nurse and told her what was happening. She took me out and held me in her hand. She told the servants to take us back to the palace. Then the Queen called the man who had made my box and had him make me a new and better box.

This box was smaller and very well made. It was only about twelve feet square and ten feet high, so that my nurse could lift it easily and could hold it on her lap. There were big windows on three sides of this box. Over each window I had the man who made it put iron bars so that the windows would not get broken.

On the fourth side, which had no window, I told him to put two big iron loops. The person who was going to carry me could put a leather belt through these loops and fasten the belt around his waist.

In this box, I had two chairs and a

table. They were made fast to the floor. I had a small bed which was also made fast to the floor. There was a hammock in which I rested when I was being taken somewhere. It was just like a hammock that a sailor sleeps in when he is on a ship at sea. I could swing from side to side in it as the carriage went over bumps. But I would not get hurt.

Now my nurse could take me out with her whenever she went for a ride. She would put a pad on her lap and put my box on the pad. I would sit on one of my chairs in front of the windows and I could see on all sides of me very well.

Sometimes the people would come close to the carriage and ask my nurse to see me. Then she would take me out in her hand and hold her hand so that all could see. She would not let anyone touch me. After a short time, she would put me back in my box and we would ride on through the city streets.

It is very hard for me to tell you what the big city in this land of Brobdingnag looks like. Everything was so big that I could not really see it the way we could see a building in England.

The walls of the buildings were a hundred feet thick and they were three thousand feet high. They were made of a beautiful white stone on which had been cut pictures of Kings and Queens and other great people.

I had a chance to measure the little finger on the hand of one of these pictures. It was longer than I was tall, which will show you how big they were. I enjoyed going on these rides with my nurse very much. But their city was too big to seem beautiful to me.

When the King and Queen saw how much I enjoyed going out, they began to take me out with them sometimes. One of the oldest, wisest servants would put my box on his belt and carry me. I went with the King and Queen to many big balls and to many dinners. They would take me when they went to visit their friends. Soon I came to be well-known in the land of Brobdingnag.

On one of these visits, the Queen heard me telling about my sea voyages. When we came back to the palace she asked me if I would not like to have a boat in which I could sail upon the water. I told her that I would like to have a boat very much. But I could not sail on any of their rivers for they ran too fast and would upset my boat.

The Queen said if I could tell the servant who had made my house how to make me a boat, she would find a place where I could sail it.

The man who had made my box was very good at making small things. I told him just how I wanted my boat made. I drew pictures of all its parts and in ten days he had made me a beautiful boat. It was big enough to hold six or eight people like me. It had oars so that I could row it.

When the Queen saw the boat she was so happy she picked it up with me inside and ran to show the King. He, too, was pleased and carefully put the boat into a bowl of water. There was not quite room enough in the big bowl for me to row as the oars were very long, but we could see that the boat was water tight.

The Queen had her servants make a big wooden tank about three hundred feet long, fifty feet wide, and eight feet deep. This was placed near a wall in one of the outer rooms of the palace. The servants filled the tank by carrying big, big buckets of water from the lake. Then my boat and I were put into the big water tank.

How the Queen and her ladies laughed when I rowed up and down this tank in my boat!

The boat also had a mast and a sail. Sometimes I would put up my sail. The ladies would make me a breeze with their fans and I would sail up and down, and from side to side as long as they were willing to fan me. When they got tired, they would call page boys to blow on my sails.

When we were all tired, my nurse would lift me out of my boat. Then she would lift the boat out of the tank of water and hang it on a nail in a closet to dry. My nurse would always be very careful about lifting me in and out of my boat. But one day, after a page boy had put my boat in the water, one of the servants picked me up to put me into the boat.

I slipped through her fingers and would have fallen forty feet to the floor if I had not caught hold of a pin on her dress. There I hung until my nurse came and lifted me off.

When the water needed to be changed in my tank, the servants brought fresh water from the lake. One time one of them took up a frog without knowing it. No one saw the frog until my boat and I were in the water, and he started to climb into the boat. He was so big he nearly turned it over. The frog was so big that he frightened me. I jumped to the other side and so kept the boat from upsetting.

When the frog got into the boat, he began jumping from end to end over my head. The water splashed into my boat! The Queen and her ladies cried for help as loudly as they could.

My nurse tried to catch the frog but in so doing she nearly upset me again. I did not want to be in the water with that awful-looking thing. I cried out to her to let me take care of him.

I took one of my oars and stood up. I hit the frog as hard as I could as he jumped over me, and knocked him into the water. Then my nurse quickly picked me out of the boat and held me safely in her hand. The page boys and servants who had come running when they heard the Queen cry, caught the frog and took him back to the lake.

I was too frightened for any more sailing that day. I never had seen such an ugly-looking thing as that frog in all my life. After that, the servants were more careful when they filled the tank with water.

The King and I used to have long talks about the differences in our countries. One day I was sitting on his dressing table talking to him while his servant shaved him.

While I watched the King, I thought of something. I asked the servant to give me some of the soap and the whiskers from the King's face. I carried this back to my box and picked the whiskers out of the soap.

My comb was broken and I knew none of these big, big people could make a comb small enough for me to use. So I thought I would try to make a comb for myself, using the King's whiskers for the teeth of the comb.

I cut a piece of wood the size I wanted my comb to be, and made it nice and smooth. Then I got a needle from my nurse and made holes in the wood.

I took my knife and sharpened the ends of the King's whiskers until they fit tightly into the needle holes. I fastened them there with little bits of wood. It made a very good comb. The King laughed when I showed him what I had made with his whiskers.

I had nothing at all to do in this country, so one day I thought of something I could make for the Queen. I had the man who made my box make me two chairs like those he had made for my house. But I asked him not to put seats or backs on them.

Then I had the Queen's ladies save me the hair that came out when they combed the Queen's hair. I took this hair and with it wove seats and backs in the chairs the way I had seen men make them from long grasses at home.

When I had them ready, I gave them to the Queen. She was very pleased with them and kept them on her dressing table to show people.

I took some more of her hair and wove a pocket-book for my nurse. It was not strong enough to hold the heavy money which she used. She just used it to carry her handkerchief.

I also learned to play the piano. I loved music, but the music they made was so loud it made my ears ache. My nurse was taking lessons on what was to them a small piano. It was about sixty feet tall and each key was about a foot wide. I could only reach five keys if I opened my arms as far as I could. I could not press one down unless I hit very hard. But I did find a way to play on this big piano.

I made two big sticks. I covered the rounded end of each one with mouse skin so I would not hurt the piano keys. I had books put under the legs of the piano bench until it was high enough so that I could hit the piano keys.

By running along on the bench and hitting the right keys with my stick I could play a little tune. This pleased my nurse very much. She called the King and Queen to hear me play a tune on the piano.

So my days passed very pleasantly in the palace of the King and Queen of Brobdingnag.

CHAPTER VII

I Get Back to England

I had now been two years in Brobdingnag. My life was very easy. But
I often thought of my wife and children
at home in England. So, when the
King and Queen said they were going
to one of their palaces by the sea, and
would take me and my nurse along,
I was very happy.

I hoped that I would see a ship from
home upon the sea, and somehow I
might get away and swim out to it.

I was carried in my box while we
were traveling. I lay in my hammock
so the bumps did not hurt me. I had
had my friend who made my box cut a
hole in the top which I could open
and shut with a stick. I could let in
some air.

My nurse and I were very tired when we came to the palace by the sea. My nurse had caught cold and she was so sick she had to be put to bed.

I grew very tired of having nothing to do. I asked the Queen if one of the page boys could take me down to the sea.

My nurse did not want me to go. But the Queen said that she thought the fresh salt air would do me good. My nurse told the page boy to be very careful of me.

The page boy carried me up and down the beach. Then I asked him to put the box down and lift me out so I could walk on the sand.

I soon found that I did not feel very well. I did not like the cold wind from the sea. I had the boy put me back inside my box and close it up tight again. I told him that I was going to take a nap.

I climbed into my hammock and went to sleep. I do not know what happened, but I think the boy must have walked away from my box.

The next thing I knew, I felt a hard pull on the ring in the top of my box which was used to lift it. I could tell that I was being lifted high, high in the air.

I called, but no one answered. I was afraid to get out of my hammock. I looked out of my windows and could see nothing but clouds and sky. All I could hear was a noise above my head like the flapping of wings.

Now I knew I was in great trouble. I felt sure that some great bird had picked up my box and that it might drop me on some rocks.

Then I heard over my head some

loud bird noises and the sound of more wings. It seemed to me that some other birds were fighting with the bird that carried my box.

All at once, I felt as if the box were falling through the air!

How frightened I was! I hung on to the sides of my hammock and expected that my box would any second be broken to pieces on the rocks. Then I would fall out of my box and be swallowed whole by one of those big birds.

Then, splash! My box hit the water and went under. I could see the green sea water through my windows. Soon the box came up to the top of the sea.

My box was partly out of the water and I could see out of the top part of my windows. The box was so well made that the water came in only at two or three little places.

Oh, how I wished I was back at the palace with my kind nurse! I knew how badly she would feel when the page boy came back and told the Queen that I had been lost.

My box was riding well upon the sea, which was quite smooth. So I lay down on my bed to rest.

I had been lying there some time when I felt my box move as if it were being pulled. I heard a noise on the outside of the wall where the loops were.

As I could not reach the top of my box from the floor, I was able to unfasten one of the chairs from the floor. I moved it over under the hole in the top of my box. This took me some time, and all the time I could feel my box moving.

As soon as I had the chair under the hole, I stood up on it and with my stick pushed back the board that closed the hole in the top of my box.

I listened and thought I could hear something that sounded like oars but could not be sure. I called for help as loudly as I could, and in all languages that I knew, but no one answered.

Then I took my stick and tied my handkerchief to the top of it. I put it out through the hole and waved it.

I could still feel my box moving and could tell by the water that I was being pulled along. Then I felt the box hit something hard and I was sure I heard a noise on the top where the ring was. I could feel that my box was being lifted. It was lifted about three feet and then it stopped.

Again I put my stick and handkerchief out of the top and cried, "Help! Help!"

This time, I heard the sound of feet

on the top of my box, and someone called, "If there is anyone in there, let him speak!"

Oh, how glad I was to hear those words, spoken in my very own language!

"I am a man from England," I cried. "Help me out of here!"

"You are safe," said the voice from outside. "Your house is fast to the side of our ship. Our carpenter will come and make a hole in the top of it to let you out."

"Oh, that will take too much time!" I said "Just have one of the sailors lift it up on deck by the ring in the top."

When I said this, the voice said, "Are you mad? It was all we could do to lift your house three feet out of the water. Just wait there. We will soon have you out.

Then I remembered that I was no

161

longer in the land of giants. These men were my size. I waited quietly while they made a hole in the top of my box, let down a ladder and helped me out.

The sailors had hundreds of questions to ask me, but I was very tired and asked to be taken to the Captain.

The Captain saw at once that I needed rest. He said we would talk later, and told me to lie down upon his bed.

Before I went to sleep, I asked him to have his men save my box. I was so tired that I forgot and asked him to just have the men bring the box into his room. I would open it and show him the things I had inside.

Since the box was much bigger than the Captain's room, he thought as the sailors had, that I was mad. He told me to lie down and sleep, which I did.

When I woke I felt much better.

The Captain gave me food and asked me to tell him what had happened.

I said, "I will be glad to do this, but it is a long story. Tell me first, how you came to find me."

The Captain said, "I first saw through my telescope the big box floating in the sea. I sent out some men in a small boat to get it.

"The men came back saying it was not a box but a floating house. I laughed at them but I went back with them myself and took a strong rope.

"When I saw that they were right, I tied my rope to the loops on your box and we pulled it back to the ship. Then we tied ropes to the ring in the top, but it was so heavy we could lift it only three feet out of the water."

I said, "Did you see any very, very big birds near where you found my box?"

He said he did, but they were so far away that they looked no bigger than most sea birds.

Then I told him my story and asked him to have his men bring in some things from my box.

He told me then that the sailors had taken everything out of the box and since they could not lift it on to the ship, they had untied it and let it float away.

The sailors brought in my things and I showed them to the Captain. I had the comb I had made from the King's whiskers, a needle my nurse had used for sewing which was a foot long, the stingers I had cut out of the wasps, some cloth I had woven from the Queen's hair, and a gold ring she had given me which I could slip on over my head like a collar.

The Captain listened to my story and

he believed me. Then he said, "I can see that you are used to talking very loudly. Were these people very hard of hearing?"

This made me laugh. I said, "No, they hear very well. But when I talked to any of them, even my nurse who was a child, it was like a man standing in the street and talking to some one up in a church steeple." After that I tried to lower my voice.

Then I told him that he and all his men looked very queer to me. I had been with giants so long that men my own size looked small and helpless to me.

We had lots of time to talk because it was many days before we got back to England. At last we sailed into the harbor I had known as a boy.

I had a hard time finding my own house, for the town had grown larger.

When I found it, my wife and daughter ran out to kiss me. They thought I acted very queerly.

When I told them my story, they began to understand and soon all was as it had been.

My wife said she was never going to let me go to sea again. I hoped that after I had been home a month or two, she would change her mind, for I was already thinking of another voyage.